This book belongs to

....

THE CLASSIC TREASURY OF

Hans Christian Andersen

ILLUSTRATED BY CHRISTIAN BIRMINGHAM
RETOLD BY MARGARET CLARK

RP|CLASSICS
PHILADELPHIA · LONDON

© 2002 by Running Press
Illustrations © 2002 by Christian Birmingham

Printed in China

Books published by Running Press are available at special discounts for bulk purchases in the United States by corporations, institutions, and other organizations. For more information, please contact the Special Markets Department at the Perseus Books Group, 2300 Chestnut Street, Suite 200, Philadelphia, PA 19103, or call (800) 810-4145, ext. 5000, or e-mail special.markets@perseusbooks.com.

9   8   7   6   5
Digit on the right indicates the number of this printing

Library of Congress Cataloging-in-Publication Number 2002100363

ISBN 978-0-7624-1393-5

Designed by Gwendolyn C. Galeone
Edited by Susan K. Hom
Typography: Minion and Poppl-Residenz

Published by Running Press Kids Classics
An Imprint of Running Press Book Publishers
A Member of the Perseus Books Group
2300 Chestnut Street
Philadelphia, PA 19103–4371

Visit us on the web!
www.runningpress.com

Contents

For
Conrad
-M.C.

Introduction

The man who originally wrote these stories described his own life as "a beautiful fairy tale." Hans Christian Andersen was born in Denmark nearly two hundred years ago. Like the ugly duckling, he was different from other children—tall and ungainly, with very large feet and long flaxen hair. His parents—a poor shoemaker and a washerwoman who couldn't read—had very little money, but they loved their son very much. They saw that he was clever and imaginative, and they encouraged his natural talent for storytelling.

His first fairy tales were published in 1835. Everyone who read them wanted more, so that soon they were translated from Danish into many other languages and Andersen became rich and famous, welcomed as an important guest in any country he wanted to visit. (He loved traveling.) He went on to write more than 150 stories. Here are eight of his best-known tales, which he wrote "exactly the way I would tell them to a child." He would read them aloud to anyone who would listen—and we hope this retelling will inspire its readers to do the same.

Thumbelina

There was once a woman who longed, above all things, for a child. No one could help her to find one, so she went to an old witch and asked what she should do.

"Take this grain of barley," said the witch, "and plant it carefully in a flowerpot."

The woman paid the witch twelve pennies and went home to plant the grain of barley. A green shoot appeared almost at once, and from it came a bud that looked as if it might be a tulip.

The woman kissed the bud and it opened instantly. There in the center of the red and yellow petals sat a child—a little girl no taller than your thumb. "I shall call you Thumbelina," said the woman.

The woman made a cradle for the little girl from half the shell of a walnut, with violet petals for the mattress and a red rose petal for the coverlet. Then she made a boat from a tulip petal which she floated in a bowl of water. She made two oars for Thumbelina out of white horsehair, and as the little girl rowed across the bowl she sang in a tiny, bell-like voice.

One night a big toad came and picked up the cradle with Thumbelina inside. While she still slept, the toad took her to the muddy bank of a stream where the toad's son was waiting. "Here is a lovely wife for you," said his mother. "Don't wake her yet; I'll put her on a water-lily leaf so that she can't run away."

Thumbelina woke next morning to find herself surrounded by water, and she wept because she didn't know how to get home again. Then up swam the mother toad

∽ Then up swam the mother toad with her son. ∽

with her son. "We've come to fetch your bed," she said. "We're going to put it in your new house, where you will be so happy with my son when he is your husband."

So they took away the walnut shell and left Thumbelina more wretched than before. Some little fishes heard her sobbing and decided she was much too beautiful to live in a mud house with an ugly toad. They found the stalk of the water-lily leaf and they ate right through it. So the leaf floated free, carrying Thumbelina down the stream.

She was so glad to have gotten away from the toads that she forgot her tears and laughed in the sunshine as a white butterfly hovered nearby. Soon it settled beside her on the leaf. Then she tied one end of the sash from her dress to the butterfly's wing and the other end to the leaf.

Now the butterfly rose quickly into the air, pulling the leaf and Thumbelina after it.

Suddenly an enormous May bug appeared. It snatched Thumbelina with her sash away from the butterfly and carried her into a tree. The May bug gave no thought to the butterfly but put Thumbelina down on another leaf and told her how beautiful she was. The lady May bugs in the tree were so jealous they made fun of her, saying how odd she was to have only two legs and no antennae. The first May bug then decided he didn't want her after all and left her on top of a daisy at the foot of the tree.

Thumbelina had to fend for herself now. She wove a hammock out of the long grass and hung it underneath a dock leaf to keep herself dry when it rained. She ate honey from the flowers and drank the morning dew.

At the end of summer, there was no more honey, and the dock leaf withered. Thumbelina was still so small that when the snow came she was almost smothered by a single snowflake. She was so cold and miserable.

Looking for some shelter, she walked into a field of stubble where she found a hole that was the entrance to a field mouse's house. The field mouse looked at her and saw how thin she was and how hungry she must be.

"Come in," the field mouse said to her. "My home underground is warm, and you can stay with me until the winter is over."

Thumbelina was grateful and promised in return to keep the field mouse entertained with a new story every day. She was not the only visitor. Next door lived a mole, who was rich and wore a black fur coat. He had a big house. The mole decided Thumbelina would make him a

good wife because he loved her singing voice. He could not see how beautiful she was, for he was blind.

The mole dug a tunnel between the mouse's home and his and suggested that she and Thumbelina could use it whenever they wanted to. He told them not to worry about a dead bird that had been buried in the tunnel. The mole did not like birds; he found their twittering irritating and thought they were stupid to let themselves starve to death in the winter.

Thumbelina remembered the birds she had seen from her water-lily leaf. She remembered their songs she had heard in the summer. When the mole took her along the tunnel, she saw that the bird, a swallow, had beautiful wings, and she felt sorry for it. That night she found some hay and took it to the tunnel to wrap round the bird. As she touched his breast, she heard a murmur and realized his heart was still beating. He was alive!

The following night Thumbelina went into the tunnel again, carrying water in a leaf. The bird drank it and said he was feel-

ing better. Then he explained how he had been left behind when all the other swallows had flown south to the warm countries to escape the frost and snow. His wing had caught in a rosebush so he could not fly with them, and the last thing he remembered was fainting in the cold.

"But now I am strong enough to fly," he said.

"No," protested Thumbelina. "It's still too cold for you."

So Thumbelina looked after him and secretly brought him food until the spring came and he could leave the mouse's home. "Come with me!" he said. "You can fly on my back." But Thumbelina knew she could not leave the field mouse who had taken her in when she was cold and homeless.

After the swallow had gone, Thumbelina was told by the field mouse that she must start weaving dresses and coats suitable for her future position as Mr. Mole's wife. Thumbelina spun her dresses by hand, while four hired spiders wove all day and night. Mr. Mole was often at the mouse's house, grumbling about the summer sunshine that made the earth so hard to dig. He was looking forward to the autumn when he would marry Thumbelina. But she could only think of how unhappy she would be living underground forever. Early in the morning, she would go up to the entrance of the mouse's home

Then they flew up into the sky, over snow-covered mountains and forests and lakes . . .

and look at the blue sky while she daydreamed about the swallow.

On the day of the wedding, Thumbelina lifted her face to the sunshine and saw in the sky above her the bird she had missed so much.

"I am so miserable," she told him. She explained how she was to marry the mole and would never see the sun again.

"This time you *must* come with me," insisted the swallow. So Thumbelina climbed onto his back and tied herself to one of his feathers. Then they flew up into the sky, over snow-covered mountains and forests and lakes, until they came to the warm countries where oranges and lemons grew. The swallow continued to fly south. Here the sun shone more brightly than Thumbelina had ever seen.

At last they came to the swallow's home, which was a nest on the white pillar of a ruined temple. The swallow came down gently onto the leaf of a white flower growing by the pillar. And there, in the center of the flower, was a man no bigger than Thumbelina. He had a crown on his head, and there were wings on his back.

The king loved Thumbelina on sight, so he took the crown off his head and put it on hers. He asked her if she would like to be queen of the flowers, and of course she said, "Yes." He was a much more suitable husband than the ugly toad or the rich mole with his black fur coat.

So they were married, and only the swallow was a little sad, for he too loved Thumbelina.

"I'm going to give you a new name," said the king. "Now you are a queen; you will be called Maia."

And the swallow said goodbye to Maia and flew back to Denmark. There he built a nest under the eaves of a house that belonged to a storyteller called Hans Christian Andersen. Whenever he sang, the man listened—and that's how we know this story.

The Nightingale

A very long time ago there was a Chinese Emperor who lived in a palace of great splendor. The walls were made of porcelain, so they were very fragile. As the Emperor's courtiers and servants moved from room to room, they had to walk with care so as not to break anything.

The palace was surrounded by pavilions where the Emperor could sit and feel the cool breezes of the evening after the sun went down. He hardly ever went into the gardens, which stretched as far as the eye could see. Beyond the gardens was a forest, and beyond the forest was the sea, where boats sailed and cormorants dived for fish.

In a tree overlooking the sea, a nightingale sang every evening at sunset, when a fisherman setting his nets would hear the bird's sweet song and say, "Thanks be to God for such a beautiful sound!"

From all over the world visitors came to see the Emperor's wonderful palace and gardens, but when they heard the nightingale, they all said this was the loveliest thing of all. After they went home they usually wrote books about all they had seen.

One of these travelers sent a copy of his book to the Emperor. As the Emperor read what had been written about the palace and its gardens, he stopped at the sentence, "But most wondrous of all is the song of the nightingale."

"The song of the nightingale?" he said. "I never knew there was a nightingale in my gardens. What you can discover by reading books!"

The Emperor summoned his chief courtier and asked

why he had never been told about this bird, which was thought to be his most wondrous possession.

"I've never heard of it," said the courtier. "It's never come to court."

"Well, it's to come now—I want to hear it sing. Everyone's heard it but me."

"No one's mentioned it to me before," said the courtier, "but I'll go and find it now."

And the courtier ran through all the rooms of the palace, asking everyone where he could find the nightingale. No one knew, so he came back to the Emperor and said it must have been a story invented by whoever had written the book.

"Your Majesty should not believe everything you read in books. Poetic fantasy is not the same as scientific observation."

The Emperor was not pleased. "That book was sent to me by the Emperor of Japan, so everything in it must be true. I want that bird here tonight. If not, every one of you shall have his stomach jumped on, just as soon as you've eaten your supper."

All of the courtiers in the room set off to find the nightingale, because none of them wanted to be jumped on. At last they came to the kitchen, where a girl was washing up pots and pans. "Are you looking for the nightingale?" she said. "I hear it every evening when I walk to the sea, to take the leftovers the cook gives me for my sick mother. It's a long walk, and I often rest for a minute or two while I listen to the nightingale's sweet song. It's so lovely that I feel as if my mother were kissing me, and I almost cry."

The chief courtier was so glad that he told the girl she could have a job for life in the kitchen if she would lead him to the nightingale.

As the crowd of courtiers followed her through the gardens and into the forest, they heard a cow bellowing.

"Oh, that's it," shouted the courtiers. "Of course we've heard it before."

"No, that's just a cow," said the girl. "We've still a long way to go to where the nightingale sings."

Farther on, the courtiers walked over a bridge across a pond where frogs were croaking.

⤳ All the courtiers looked up at the small bird sitting on a branch of magnolia blossoms. ⤳

"What a lovely sound!" cried the courtiers. "Just like church bells ringing."

"No, that's only the frogs," said the girl. "But we are getting close to where the nightingale sings."

And at that moment, the nightingale's voice could be heard.

"There!" said the girl. "Look and listen."

All the courtiers looked up at the small bird sitting on a branch of magnolia blossoms.

"How can that be?" said the chief courtier. "Such a dull and insignificant bird. Perhaps it's lost its color because it's embarrassed to be facing so many noble people like us."

"Nightingale!" shouted the girl. "Our Emperor wants you to sing for him."

"Delighted," called back the nightingale, and he began his song again.

"Why have we never heard this beautiful sound before?" said the chief courtier. "And where does it come from? Let's watch the bird's throat."

"Would the Emperor like another song?" asked the nightingale, who thought the Emperor was in the crowd.

"Most talented little nightingale," said the chief courtier, "I am inviting you to come with us to the Emperor's palace tonight, where His Majesty wishes you to sing for him."

"My voice really does sound best out of doors," said the nightingale, but he followed the courtiers back to the palace.

There all the rooms had been decorated with scented flowers hung with silver bells. The porcelain walls and tiled floors were lit by thousands of little golden lamps. The Emperor was standing before his throne in the banqueting hall, and nearby was a golden perch ready for the nightingale. The girl from the kitchen who had found the nightingale was told she could stand behind one of the doors to listen.

When the nightingale began to sing, the sound was so beautiful that tears came to the Emperor's eyes. He had never heard such a lovely song, and he gave the little bird the best reward he could think of. The Emperor's golden slipper was hung round the bird's neck.

"Thank you," said the nightingale. "But I have my reward already—the tears on your cheeks. To make an Emperor cry at the sound of my song is the greatest honor I could wish for."

Everyone was enchanted by the nightingale. The ladies of the court even tried to imitate his song by filling their mouths with water and making rippling noises.

Whenever he left his golden perch, he was followed by four servants, each holding one of four silk ribbons tied to his legs. He didn't like this very much.

One day another present arrived from the Emperor of Japan. It was a toy nightingale made of gold and silver. Its feathers were decorated with precious jewels, and in its back was a little golden key. When the key was turned, the bird sang and its silver tail moved up and down.

"What a magnificent bird!" said the chief courtier. "Why don't we make the two nightingales sing a duet together?" But the two birds couldn't keep time together, because the real nightingale sang from his heart, and the toy nightingale did not have a heart—only a clock-work cylinder.

"This one keeps perfect time," said the royal music master, "just like my best pupils."

So the toy nightingale sang by itself in a golden cage, and the courtiers all agreed its song was just as beautiful as the song of the real nightingale. And it was so sumptuous to look at—all its precious jewels glistened in the lamplight.

The toy nightingale repeated its song thirty-three times, and of course, it never grew tired. The courtiers would have gone on listening forever, but the Emperor called for the real nightingale to take his turn. Then there was silence—for no one had seen him flying home to the green forest.

"Who let him go?" thundered the Emperor—but everyone blamed the nightingale himself.

"Never mind," said the royal music master. "We still have the best bird. See how finely the toy nightingale has been programmed, to produce the perfect song time after time. You can never rely on the real nightingale. Who knows what he will sing or when?"

All the courtiers clapped, and the Emperor announced that he would let the toy nightingale sing for

Then there was silence—for no one had seen him flying home to the green forest.

the people who lived outside the palace walls.

They all loved its song, but the fisherman who had heard the real nightingale while he set his nets was puzzled. "That *sounds* like a nightingale," he said to himself. "But I know something is not quite right."

The toy nightingale was given a place of honor at the Emperor's bedside, while the real nightingale was banished from his empire. Every time the toy nightingale sang, more presents arrived. The royal music master wrote a long thesis about its song, which no one could understand but dared not say so.

Then one day a dreadful thing happened. As the toy nightingale started to sing, something inside it went "Snap!" and the music stopped. The royal watchmaker took the bird to bits and put it together again. He shook his head sadly and announced that it could never be repaired properly. It might be able to sing once a year, but it might not get to the end of its song.

Some years later an even more dreadful thing happened. The Emperor became ill. He stayed in bed all day, and everyone believed he was going to die. The tiles on the floors of the palace were covered with black carpets so that no footstep should disturb him.

As the Emperor grew weaker, he saw the figure of Death sitting by his bed, already wearing the crown and sword that were his. The Emperor was very frightened and called out, "Oh my friend, little nightingale, please sing for me!"

But the toy nightingale had no heart and no voice, and the silence in the palace was complete.

Then from outside the window came the most beautiful sound in all the world. It was the real nightingale who, hearing of the Emperor's plight, had returned to comfort him. The Emperor felt his blood quickening, and the figure of Death began to fade. As the nightingale sang of a churchyard where mourners' tears made the grass green and the roses fragrant, Death put aside the Emperor's crown and sword and disappeared.

"Oh, nightingale," murmured the Emperor, "how can I thank you enough?"

"I have not forgotten your tears when I first sang for you," said the nightingale. "They were my most precious reward."

Then the Emperor slept, and the next morning he was better. The real nightingale was still singing from his branch outside the window.

"Please stay," said the Emperor. "I won't ask you for anything. You need only sing when you want to. I will smash the toy bird into a thousand pieces."

"No, no," said the real nightingale. "The toy bird did what it had been made to do. I can't live in your palace like it did. My home is in the open air. But I will come often to see you. I will sing you songs about all the things you can't see from your porcelain palace—the fisherman who sets his nets in the sea at the end of your garden, the girl who walks so far to visit her sick mother. If I do that, you must give me a promise."

"Anything," said the Emperor.

"You must never tell anyone that it is a nightingale who tells you these things." And the little bird flew away.

When his courtiers came into the bedroom, expecting to find him dead, the Emperor, dressed in his finest robes, said cheerfully, "Good morning!"

The Steadfast Tin Soldier

There was once a boy who was given a box of tin soldiers for his birthday. He was so pleased that he took them out of their box straightaway and set them out on parade. All twenty-four of them stood to attention, their red and blue Danish uniforms immaculate, each with his rifle held on his right shoulder. Only one was not perfect. He stood on one leg, because there had not been enough tin to make him two.

The boy also had a toy castle made of cardboard, which he kept on the table that was covered with his toys. The mistress of the castle was a ballet dancer who stood at the entrance poised on the toes of one leg while the other was held high under her skirt of white muslin. She was made of paper, except for her skirt and a blue ribbon fastened by a large silver spangle over her shoulder.

The tin soldier with one leg looked at the little dancer, who seemed also to have only one leg and thought what a perfect couple they would make. "But I am not good enough for her," he said to himself. "She lives in a castle, and I have to share a box with twenty-three other soldiers. Even so, I'd like to get to know her."

That night, when everyone in the house was asleep, the toys woke up and started to play. Only the tin soldiers, fastened in their box, could not join in. But the soldier with one leg had hidden himself behind a snuffbox, so that he could gaze at the ballerina. While the other toys played hide-and-seek and made an awful noise, the ballerina remained on her toes, absolutely still, and the tin soldier never took his eyes off her.

When the clock struck midnight, the snuffbox flew

The next morning the boy was playing with the tin soldier and stood him on the windowsill.

open and out sprang a troll. "Tin soldier!" he shouted. "Stop staring!"

The tin soldier took no notice.

"Just you wait," said the troll and snapped back into his box.

The next morning the boy was playing with the tin soldier and stood him on the windowsill. Who knows whether the troll had anything to do with what happened next. Suddenly the tin soldier was out of the window and falling down three stories to the street. The boy rushed downstairs and outside to find him but could not see him. The tin soldier didn't cry out, because he thought that would be undignified when he was in uniform. So the boy went back into the house, and the tin soldier lay forlorn in the street, his bayonet wedged in the dirt between two cobblestones.

A shower of rain filled the gutter, and two boys, passing, made a paper boat and put the tin soldier on board. The water ran fast and the boat tossed and turned, so that the tin

soldier was quite frightened, but he stood as steadfast as ever, his rifle at his shoulder. The gutter ran into a tunnel, and now the tin soldier was in the dark. He heard a voice. It was a rat shouting, "Where's your passport? Show me your papers!" The tin soldier said nothing and looked ahead grimly. There was light at the end of the tunnel, but he could now hear the dreadful sound of water falling. It was running into one of the canals in the city's harbor.

As the boat went over the edge into the canal, the tin soldier knew he was going to drown. He thought of the ballerina and said to himself, "If this is my fate, then I will meet it like the bold warrior that I am."

The paper boat collapsed, and at that very moment a fish opened its mouth and swallowed the tin soldier whole. He lay in the darkness of the fish's stomach still holding his rifle with his right hand.

The next minute, it seemed, there was light and someone was saying, "Look, it's a tin soldier!" The fish had been sold in the market, and the kitchen maid had opened it up before cooking it.

The tin soldier was carried into a room where, to his amazement, he saw twenty-three other tin soldiers, a castle and, standing on one leg, the ballerina. He looked at her, and she gazed back. They did not speak.

Maybe the troll heard what was happening from inside his snuff-box; maybe he was just being mischievous; but for some reason, one of the children took it into his head to grab the tin soldier and throw him into the stove. The tin soldier was still standing upright as the flames

touched his uniform, and he went on gazing at the ballerina as his body melted.

Someone walked into the room, and through the open door came a draught that caught the ballerina's skirt and blew her into the stove. She was gone quickly as the tin soldier continued to melt. All that was left the next morning was the little tin soldier's tin heart and the spangle from the ballerina's blue ribbon. It had turned black as coal.

The Little Mermaid

Deep down in the ocean, where no diver has ever been, there is a castle built of coral where the king of the mer-people once lived. His wife had died soon after the youngest of her six daughters was born. The princesses were all very beautiful, but, like every other mermaid, they did not walk on two feet but swam with their long fishtails. The loveliest princess was the youngest: she had skin like a rose petal and eyes of deepest blue.

The princesses were happy playing with the fishes that came into the castle through the amber windows, but best of all they enjoyed looking after their own little gardens in the park surrounding the castle. The strangest flowers and trees grew under the sea in the sand that was blue like the sky above, and sometimes you could see the red sun shining through the water.

The princesses could put what they liked in their gardens, so among the plants were all kinds of odd things they had collected from shipwrecks. The youngest princess had only one: the statue of a human boy made out of translucent marble. Next to it she planted a pink tree, rather like a weeping willow, whose branches fell on the blue sand.

The youngest princess knew that the boy came from a very different world above the sea. Her old grandmother would often tell her stories about human beings, their ships and their homes, and the animals that lived on land. What sounded most wonderful were the flowers that had a sweet scent (the flowers under water had none) and the "fishes" in the trees that could sing. Grandmother called them "fishes" because the princess did not know what a bird was.

Grandmother promised that when each princess reached her fifteenth birthday, she would be allowed to leave the castle and go up to look at the world on land from a rock close to the shore. The youngest was only ten when the eldest returned to tell the others of all she had seen during her day above the water. She had watched lights come on in the big city as darkness fell; she had heard human beings talking to one another. She had listened to the sound of music. She had heard church bells ringing.

The smallest princess longed for the time to pass until she could hear such sounds. Now she could only dream of what she would see.

For the second princess, the most beautiful sight had been the sunset, with a golden sky and clouds of crimson. Swans had crossed the sky just as the sun sank below the horizon.

The third princess left the sea and swam up a river, where she saw fields and hills, woods and farms. She met children, who were frightened by the sight of her fishtail, and a black dog, who didn't like it either and barked at her furiously.

The fourth princess didn't go near the shore. She had seen greater marvels on the surface of the sea—dolphins leaping and huge whales spouting water high into the sky.

The fifth princess went to the surface in winter and found icebergs as high as the church towers in the city. She climbed onto the largest one and watched the lightning flash as a storm arose. Sailors on ships took down their sails and clung to the masts in fear.

All five sisters, having seen the world above, realized that their father's castle was the place they loved and regarded as home. But often they would swim together to the surface of the sea and sing to the sailors, who thought they were listening to the wind. The sixth princess longed to go with them and felt like weeping when she couldn't, but mermaids cannot cry and that makes them even more miserable.

"I want so much to be fifteen," she said. "I want to

And seated in the boat was a young man, a prince, with dark eyes and a beaming smile.

see the world above, and I know I shall love those who live there."

At last her birthday came, and her grandmother dressed her carefully. She put lilies in her hair and eight oysters on her tail.

"They're pinching me," said the princess, but her grandmother insisted that she must be seen to be a real princess.

When she came to the surface of the sea, it was early evening. There in the fading light she saw a ship, quite still on a calm sea. On the deck, under hundreds of tiny lamps hanging from the rigging, was a crowd of people looking towards a boat making its way to the side of the ship. And seated in the boat was a young man, a prince, with dark eyes and a beaming smile. As he stepped onto the ship, a hundred rockets flew up into the sky, for it was his sixteenth birthday.

The little princess was afraid she would be seen in the light that glistened on the water, but everyone was looking at the prince. He greeted every one of the sailors, and they all began to dance to hornpipe music as more fireworks shot into the heavens. How the little mermaid wanted to join them! But she could only watch—until the fireworks were finished and the tiny lamps all put out.

It was midnight and, as the little mermaid swam to and fro, she could feel the sea start to boil and swirl beneath her. A storm was coming. The ship tossed and turned on the waves, and its timbers groaned as they took the force of the water. There was a terrible cracking sound.

The little mermaid saw that the tall mast had broken in two—and the ship overturned. The sea was suddenly full of bits of wood and bodies of young men trying to find something to hang onto. But where was the prince? Perhaps, thought the little mermaid, he was already on his way to her father's castle—but then she remembered that he could not live under the water as she could. "Oh, don't let him die!" she said to herself, and at that moment she caught sight of him, still trying to swim to safety but too tired to stay afloat.

The little mermaid put her arms round him and held his head above the water. The waves carried them away from the shipwreck, and what happened to the others, the little mermaid never knew. When dawn came, the prince's eyes were still closed, and he looked like the marble statue

in the little mermaid's garden. She kissed him again and again and willed him to live.

At last they came to land. There was a garden with lemon and orange trees and beyond it buildings, from which came the sound of bells ringing and girls laughing. The little mermaid gently pulled the prince's body onto the sand at the edge of the water and laid his head where the sun could warm his pale cheeks.

There she had to leave him. She watched as he opened his eyes when the girls discovered him and carried him indoors.

Now she knew he was probably alive, but she could only swim home to her father's castle. She was silent when her sisters asked what she had seen on her first visit to the world above.

All she could think about was the prince, and often she would go back to the place where she had left him. She never saw him, and she became so sad that she neglected her garden and went into it only to kiss the statue which so reminded her of him.

Her sisters at last persuaded her to tell them why she

was so unhappy. Then they found out where the prince had his kingdom, from another mermaid who had also watched his birthday party on the ship. So they took the little mermaid, and they found the wonderful palace where the prince lived. Its rooms were hung with tapestries, and in its central hall was a fountain with a glass dome, through which the sunlight sparkled.

The little mermaid was content just to be able to watch the prince when he came out of his palace to walk in the gardens or to sail his boat. She began to think about his life as a human being and asked her grandmother, "If a sailor doesn't drown after a shipwreck, does he ever die, like my mother did?"

"Men die just as we do," said her grandmother, "but

they don't live as long as we do. We mer-people can live to be three hundred years old, but when we die, we are gone forever, we are no more than the spray on the sea. Men have souls that are immortal. When their bodies die, their souls live on in a world as yet unknown to them, a world we could never reach."

"I don't want to die," said the little mermaid, "and be nothing. Why can't I have a soul?"

"No mermaid has a soul," said her grandmother, "but if a man loved you so much that he put his hand in yours before a priest and promised never to leave you, then part of his soul could become yours. And that will never happen. No man would love you, because you have a fishtail."

The little mermaid was inconsolable. While her sisters danced and sang at a ball given for them by the mer-king, she could think only of the prince in the world above, for whom she would do anything.

Then she remembered the sea witch, who lived far from the castle beyond a forest of trees with strange, slimy branches. The little mermaid swam as fast as she could to the witch's house. The witch was sitting at the door with eels playing on her lap. She beckoned the little mermaid to follow her inside.

"I know why you have come, you silly girl," said the witch. "You want to exchange your fishtail for two stumpy legs so that the prince will love you. If you really want that, I can make you a potion that will give you legs as beautiful as a dancer's, but the pain will be terrible when your new feet touch the ground. Are you ready to face that?"

"Oh yes," said the little mermaid faintly.

"That's not all," the witch said nastily. "Once your tail is gone, you can never be a mermaid again. If the prince does not love you so much that he will put his hand in yours before a priest and promise never to leave you, then when he marries someone else, you will die of a broken heart."

"I am not afraid," said the little mermaid.

"There's a price, too," said the witch.

"The potion is made from my very own blood, so that you must give me your most precious possession, and that's your voice."

With that the witch mixed the potion. When it was done, she gave it to the little mermaid and removed her tongue.

Now she could never return to her father's castle,

⌒ With that the witch mixed the potion. ⌒

because she could not tell her sisters why she was leaving them. Instead she swam to the prince's palace and sat on the marble steps while she drank the potion. The pain was so bad that she fainted, and when she opened her eyes, there, looking down at her, was the prince himself. Where her fishtail had been were two long legs and two tiny feet.

The prince led her into his palace, and every step was painful, as the witch had warned. But she smiled, because she was so glad to be at the prince's side, although she could answer none of his questions about where she had come from. He had her dressed in fine silk and became so fond of her that he let her sleep on velvet pillows outside his bedroom door. But often she would wake and go down to the sea to cool her aching feet.

Every day the little mermaid tried to tell him with her eyes, "I love you so much—don't you love me too?" and at last the prince explained why he liked to have her near him.

"You remind me of a girl I shall never see again. I had been washed ashore when my ship was wrecked. She found me, and I was taken into the cloister where she lives with other girls, shut away from the world. Now I can look at you and think of her."

The little mermaid sadly remembered how she had rescued the prince and left him on the shore where the cloister stood, but she could never tell him what had really happened.

One day the prince's parents arranged for him to visit a nearby kingdom. Everyone knew that they wanted him

to marry the princess who lived there, but he told the little mermaid he could not do that—he loved only the girl from the cloister. And he kissed the little mermaid because she reminded him of that girl, and the little mermaid dreamed of him putting his hand in hers before a priest, and promising never to leave her.

When the prince arrived in the nearby kingdom, there were great celebrations but no sign of the princess. The prince became impatient, but when she came at last he was overjoyed. "You are the girl who rescued me!" he cried. She had been sent to the cloister to learn her royal duties.

The little mermaid knew now that on the wedding day her heart would break and she would die.

She smiled bravely as she carried the train of the

they seemed to be part of the sky. "Who are you?" she called, and knew that her voice had come back.

"We are daughters of the air." The answer was like a whisper on the wind. "We are not mermaids, who can only win an immortal soul when they are loved by a human being. We can earn souls by doing good. And you, little mermaid, have tried to do good—you rescued the prince; you spared him when you could have killed him with a knife. So you are now one of us. Go on doing good, and after three hundred years you will be given an immortal soul."

The little mermaid looked for the last time at the prince's ship, where she could see the prince and his princess searching for her. Serenely she followed the daughters of the air up into the sky. "In three hundred years," she said, "I shall see eternity."

"That time may come sooner," her companions replied. "When we fly into the homes of human beings, we look for the children. If they have been good, a year is taken from the time we have to earn immortality. But if the children have behaved badly, then we cry—for an extra day is added to the three hundred years before we have our reward."

bride's dress and watched the prince put his hand in hers. Then they all went on board the prince's ship to sing and dance until midnight. The little mermaid remembered how she had watched the prince's birthday party on the ship the first time she had come to the surface of the sea.

So she danced with a heavy heart, knowing that the next morning she would die. When the party ended and all were asleep, she stood at the rail of the ship, and in the sea she saw her five sisters swimming towards her. Their heads were bare.

"We have given our hair to the sea witch in exchange for this knife. She says that if you kill the prince before the sun rises and let his blood touch your feet, then you will be a mermaid again, and you can live happily with us for three hundred years."

The little mermaid took the knife and went to the prince's bed, where he and his princess lay sleeping. As the sun rose, she kissed him once and threw the knife far out into the sea. Quickly she slipped off the ship, feeling as light as air. Then above her she saw shapes so transparent

As the sun rose, she kissed him once and threw the knife far out into the sea.

The Little Match Girl

It was New Year's Eve. The snow was falling on streets now empty of people, for it was almost dark. Everyone had gone home to bank up fires and prepare a feast to celebrate the end of the old year. Only a little girl was left—and she seemed to have nowhere to go. She had lost both her shoes: they had been her mother's, and too big for her, and they had come off as she ran out of the way of two carriages dashing along the road. Her feet were dirty and scratched: they looked almost frozen. Her long yellow hair was covered with snowflakes. She had no coat—just a thin dress and apron.

In the apron, she carried a bundle of matches, which she had been trying to sell all day. No one had bought a single match from her, and now she could not go home because her father would beat her if she returned empty-handed. She was cold, hungry, and wretched.

She thought about the people who lived in the well-lit houses she passed. She thought about them sitting round the fire, warming their toes. She thought about the goose roasting on the spit, which she could smell from the street. She thought about the cold attic where she lived, under a roof that did not keep out the wind because it was full of holes.

She could suddenly bear no more, and she slumped to the ground in an alleyway between two houses. She took one of her matches and struck it on the brick wall. She held her other hand round its bright flame and felt its warmth. Then it grew bigger and for a moment she seemed to be sitting in front of a big iron stove. Oh, how blissful it was . . . but as she put out her legs to warm them,

≈ Only a little girl was left—and she seemed to have nowhere to go. ≈

the picture disappeared. She was as cold as ever, with a spent match in her hand.

She had wasted one match; she might as well strike another. This time the flame sprang up so quickly the wall seemed to melt away, and she looked into a room where the table was spread for a wonderful meal. The tablecloth was sparkling white, and the china was of the most delicate colors, rimmed with gold. On a great platter in the middle of the table lay a fat goose, its stuffing of apples and prunes giving off a smell that made her mouth water. As she gazed inside, the goose got to its feet, jumped off the table, and walked towards her. But before it reached her, all went dark again, and her hands felt only the bitter cold of the wall.

Almost fainting with hunger, the little girl struck her third match. Now above her she could see a Christmas tree that was bigger and more beautifully decorated than any she had ever seen before. Thousands of candles flickered in its branches, but as she marveled at them, the match went out. Instead of the candles on a tree, she saw the stars far away in the heavens. One of them shot across the sky.

"That means someone is dying," she thought. Her dead grandmother, who'd been the only one to love her, had explained that when a star falls, it means a human soul is on its way to God.

The little girl struck another match, and in its light she saw her grandmother, just as she remembered her, smiling with such warm kindness. "Grandmother!" she called out. "Don't go away like the stove and the goose and the Christmas tree. Let me come with you!"

She lit all the matches that were left so there was light everywhere, and her grandmother came nearer. She hugged the little girl and carried her away from the cold street, up into the arms of God.

The next morning the little girl lay dead, her body frozen, yet her face at peace. In her apron were all the spent matches. The people who found her said, "She must have been trying to keep warm." No one realized what visions her matches had brought; no one knew how she and her grandmother had greeted the New Year.

The Emperor's New Clothes

A long time ago there lived an Emperor who was so vain that he spent hours every day changing his clothes and looking at himself in the mirror. He wasn't interested in his soldiers, who marched up and down in front of his palace. He didn't care about the musicians and actors who worked so hard to amuse him at the theater. He thought that driving in the park was boring. The only thing that made him happy was buying new clothes.

His palace stood in the middle of a large and busy town. One day two tricksters walked into the marketplace. They announced to the crowd that gathered round them that they were weavers. The cloth they could weave was the finest to be found anywhere in the world—but only people who were clever and good at their jobs could actu-

ally see it. To all those who were stupid and incompetent, it was completely invisible.

When the Emperor heard this, he was very excited. "If I get some new clothes made of this material, I shall know which of my councillors are clever and which I should get rid of," he thought. So he gave the tricksters all the money they asked for and told them to start weaving.

The two men brought their looms into the palace and pretended to set to work. Sitting at the looms, they moved their hands to and fro, but what had they done with the fine silks and gold thread they insisted the Emperor should buy for them? He so much wanted to know how they were getting on, but he dare not go into the room where they were working for fear that he would not be able to see the wonderful material they were weaving.

That would mean he was really stupid. He decided to send his prime minister instead, for he was quite sure that this man was very clever.

The prime minister, who was old and good-natured, went along happily to watch the weavers. "Goodness me," he said to himself. "I can't see any cloth." The weavers smiled and invited him to come closer so that he could examine the exquisite detail of their work. The prime minister stared, opening his eyes as wide as he could. "Am I so stupid?" he thought. "Surely not . . . yet perhaps I'm not a very good prime minister. I'd better not admit I can't see what they are doing."

"Do tell us what you think," said one of the tricksters.

"The cloth is beautiful," stammered the prime minister nervously. "How *did* you create such colors and pat-

terns? I must report to the Emperor at once."

The tricksters smiled even more and spent a long time describing the intricate patterns and mixture of colors they had put into the cloth. The prime minister listened to all they said and repeated it faithfully to the Emperor. The Emperor believed everything his prime minister told him, so he agreed at once when the tricksters asked for more money and more gold thread.

The next day the Emperor was even more anxious to know how the work was progressing, and he sent one of his privy councillors to have a look. This man went up to the looms and, of course, he saw nothing.

"Now don't you think that is the finest piece of cloth you have ever seen?" asked one of the tricksters.

"Goodness me," said the privy councillor to himself.

Not one of them could see any cloth, but they all said, "It is beautiful . . ."

"I know I'm not stupid, but if I can't see the cloth, perhaps I'll lose my job. I'd better not admit that I can't see a thing." So out loud he told the tricksters it was the finest piece of cloth he had ever seen—and went straight back to the Emperor and repeated his words.

By now everyone knew about the wonderful cloth the tricksters were weaving, and, at last, the Emperor could wait no longer. Accompanied by his prime minister, his privy councillor, and his courtiers, he went to the room where the weavers still sat at their empty looms.

"Look, isn't that magnificent?" said the prime minister.

"Observe the detail in the work," said the privy councillor.

The Emperor was horrified. "Why can't I see it?" he thought. "I must be stupid. Perhaps I'm not such a good Emperor after all. I can't bear this." Aloud he said, "It is . . . er . . . beautiful."

The prime minister, the privy councillor, and the courtiers all stared at the looms. Not one of them could see any cloth, but they all said, "It *is* beautiful. Your Majesty, why don't you have a suit of new clothes made from this exquisite material?"

The two tricksters were now appointed Royal Knights of the Looms and were commanded to have the Emperor's new clothes ready for his next procession through the town. They worked all night to finish the royal suit of clothes. They cut the invisible material with their big scissors; they sewed the pieces together with invisible thread. And when they had finished, they asked if the Emperor would like to try on his new clothes.

"You will feel as if you are not wearing any clothes at all," one of the tricksters said. "The material is so light and delicate."

"It's like nothing we have seen before," said the courtiers, who could indeed see nothing.

"Will you go to the mirror, Your Majesty?" asked the tricksters. "If we may take off your clothes, we will help you to put the new ones on."

So the Emperor stood in front of the mirror, and the tricksters pretended to dress him, tying round his waist an invisible train to be carried by the two noblest courtiers.

Then everyone gazed at the Emperor and began to pay him compliments. "What a perfect fit!" said one. "Those new clothes suit you so well!" said another.

The Emperor looked at himself in the mirror, and, although all he could see was bare flesh, he pretended to be as pleased with his new clothes as any he'd ever had before.

Outside the palace waited the silk canopy under which the Emperor was to walk in the procession. When he was ready, the courtiers who were to carry his train fell over themselves in their efforts to find it, because, of course, it wasn't there. At last they were settled, holding up their hands to carry the invisible train.

As the procession began to move, the crowds lining the streets waved and shouted. They could all see that the Emperor was wearing his crown, yet no one dared admit to being so stupid that they could see he wasn't wearing any clothes. "What beautiful cloth!" they called. "What wonderful new clothes!"

But high above the crowds, perched on a lamppost, was a child who shouted, "Look! There's a man with nothing on!"

His father said, "Listen to what my little boy says." And, one by one, people in the crowds passed the message on, until they all cried, "There's a man with nothing on!"

The Emperor heard their cries and knew in his heart that the people were right. But he thought to himself, "I must behave as if nothing were wrong." And he walked firmly ahead, while the courtiers continued to carry the royal train that wasn't there.

Perched on a lamppost was a child who shouted, "Look! There's a man with nothing on!"

The *Ugly Duckling*

A duck once built her nest under the cover of some burdock leaves near the moat of an old castle. There she laid her eggs and sat patiently, waiting for them to hatch. Although she liked the nest, which was shaded from the heat of midsummer, the mother duck missed the company of her friends, who swam about, gossiping in the moat.

At last she heard a tapping and a cracking. Out of the eggs came the little ducklings, who were squeaking with excitement at seeing the world around them.

"Quack! Quack!" said the mother duck. "How glad I am that you're here. But is this all of you? Oh, don't say that big egg hasn't hatched yet. I am so bored with sitting on it."

"Let me have a look," said an old duck who was pass-ing by. "Now that's a turkey egg. You are going to have a lot of trouble with it. Turkeys don't like water. I would just leave it and take the others to the moat to learn how to swim."

But the mother duck felt she couldn't abandon that last egg, so she waited until there was an even noisier tap-ping and cracking. Out of the biggest egg came the biggest bird, who was also very ugly.

The mother duck was shocked. "I suppose he must be a turkey," she thought and decided to find out by taking her whole family to the moat.

The little ducklings followed each other into the water and seemed to know without being told how to pad-dle with their legs and stay afloat. Even the ugly duckling could do it.

"He doesn't look like us!" the others retorted, laughing at him.

"He can't be a turkey," said his mother. "He knows exactly how to use his legs and how to hold his head up. So I can be just as proud of him as I am of the rest. I am going to take all of you to the farmyard to show you off."

When the family reached the farmyard, the mother duck told her ducklings how they were to behave. "Remember to walk with your legs far apart. That's the way we ducks walk. It's called waddling. And remember always to bow to the old duck in that corner. She comes from a very old family. That red rag is tied round her leg so that everyone can recognize her and bow their heads to her."

The ducklings did what they were told, but other ducks made fun of them. One bit the ugly duckling in the neck.

"Go away!" shouted his mother. "He hasn't done you any harm."

"He doesn't look like us!" the others retorted. "That's a good enough reason to bite him."

The old, fat duck with the red rag stepped nearer. "All your children are good-looking except this one. Why can't you put him back in the egg and start again?"

"I couldn't do that," said his mother. "And really he's a good son and swims well. His looks may improve as he grows up."

But the ugly duckling knew he was different from the others, and the more all the hens and ducks chased and laughed at him, the more miserable he became. The real turkey cock made a gobbling noise at him, and he shook with fright.

His brothers and sisters wished the cat would get him so they could be rid of him. Even his mother secretly wanted him to go away. So one day he did. He flew out of the farmyard and waddled as far as he could.

He spent the night in a swamp, where he was found by some wild ducks. "Who are you?" they said. The poor ugly duckling didn't know who he was, but he bowed to them all, knowing this was polite. "Well, ugly one," they said, "you can stay with us for a while; just don't think of marrying into our family."

The ugly duckling didn't want to marry; he only wanted a place to swim and water to drink.

The next day two wild ganders befriended him. "Come with us," they said. "You *are* ugly, but we don't mind that."

The next moment there was the sound of gunshot, and both wild ganders fell dead. Hunters and dogs came crashing through the swamp. The ugly duckling was so terrified that he lay still on the ground with his head under his wing.

The hunters went on shooting for several hours. The ugly duckling dare not move until he was sure they had gone far away. Then he moved as fast as he could out of the swamp, through woods and fields, until he came to a hut, so old that it seemed to be swaying in the wind. The ugly duckling crept inside and fell asleep. He was found in the morning by the old woman who lived in the hut with her cat and her hen. They were not very pleased to see him, but the old woman said he could stay because she did not know he was a drake and thought he would lay eggs for her.

The hen said suspiciously, "Can you lay eggs?" And when the duckling said, "No," replied, "Then keep quiet about it."

The cat said, "Can you arch your back like I can? Can you purr?"

"No," said the duckling, and the cat replied that he had no right to chatter on about what he wanted when others were making intelligent conversation. The

duckling had been saying how much he missed the moat and how wonderful it was to dive to the bottom and get his head wet.

"That sounds cool," said the hen dryly. "I can't imagine that the cat would like to dive to the bottom of a moat, but why not ask him? He's not stupid. Or ask the old woman if she would like to go in the water and get her hair wet."

"You don't understand what I mean," whined the duckling.

"Now I hope you're not saying you're more intelligent than we are. Be grateful you've found a place where people can teach you something. Stop talking nonsense and learn how to lay eggs or arch your back and purr. I'm saying this for your own good, remember."

"I think I'll be on my way," said the ugly duckling.

"Please yourself," said the hen.

So the ugly duckling went on his own way again. He

discovered a place to live beside a lake where he could dive to the bottom and get his head wet. The other ducks there took no notice of him because he was so ugly.

One autumn evening, he saw some birds he had never seen before. They had the whitest of feathers, long

elegant necks, and enormous wings. They flew together in a massive white cloud and made a piercing cry. The duckling did not know they were swans, flying south to the warm countries where the lakes do not freeze in winter. The duckling loved them on sight; he wanted to go with them, yet he was content with what he had—a small space in the lake that wasn't yet frozen. He swam round and round as the weather grew colder until he was finally stuck fast in the ice. A farmer rescued him and took him into the warm farm kitchen. The farmer's children thought it would be fun to play with him, but he took fright and flew round the kitchen, falling into a bucket of milk, struggling out of there onto the butter and ending up in a barrel of flour. The duckling now looked uglier than ever, and the children chased him out of the house into the snow, where he hid and thought his life was done.

Somehow he survived the snow and ice, and when spring arrived, he felt ready to fly again. He found his way to a garden where the apple trees were in flower. Lilac bushes fringed the water of a canal, and suddenly on to the water came three swans. The ugly duckling recognized them and thought to himself, "I must go to those birds. When they see how ugly I am, they will probably bite me, but what does it matter? I'd rather be killed by those beautiful creatures than bitten by ducks or shot by hunters or frozen by winter."

So the ugly duckling swam towards the swans, who turned to meet him. "Do what you like with me," he said, bending his head. And looking at his reflection in the water, he saw not an ungainly, overgrown, and ugly duckling, but a swan! He had been born in a duck's nest but had come out of a swan's egg.

He was so happy—all the more so because he had known such misery until now. The three swans swam round him and touched him lovingly with their beaks.

Children came to feed the swans with bread and cake. Seeing a newcomer, they looked at him closely and said he was the most handsome of them all. As he listened to the children shouting and laughing, he remembered the times he had been bullied and pecked. Now everyone had kind words for him, the sun was shining, and the lilac bushes seemed to bend over the water just to be near him. He stretched his neck up in the air and thought, "I never dreamt of such joy when I was only the ugly duckling."

"I never dreamt of such joy when I was only the ugly duckling."

The Princess and the Pea

There was once a prince who wanted a wife. But not just any girl would do—she had to be a real princess. So he set off round the world, visiting the royal families of all the kingdoms he could find—and every princess he met wanted to marry him, but not one of them lived up to his dream of what a princess should be.

When he had seen them all, the prince came home and felt very sad and lonely.

One night there was a flash of lightning in the sky, followed quickly by a crash of thunder, and then—down came the rain! It made so much noise that only the prince's father, the king, heard a knock at the palace door. When he opened it, there stood a girl, who was shivering with cold and very, very wet. Her long hair was dripping down her back like rats' tails, and her clothes clung to her.

Her toes squelched in her shoes as she stamped her feet, trying to get warm.

"Please let me in," she said. "I know the prince will be glad to see me, because I'm a real princess."

"Well, we'll soon find out," thought the queen to herself, as she hurried the girl to the fire to take off her wet clothes.

While the girl warmed herself, the queen went to make up the bed for her in the palace's guest room. First she looked in a kitchen cupboard for one tiny dried pea, and then she placed it carefully in the middle of the bare bedstead. Next, on top of the pea, she put the mattress, and another, and another—until there were twenty mattresses in the pile. Then she fetched twenty eiderdowns stuffed with the softest duck feathers and threw those up

The girl was so tired that she thought she would fall asleep the moment she closed her eyes.

one by one on top of the mattresses. The girl was so tired that she thought she would fall asleep the moment she closed her eyes.

Next morning, at breakfast, the queen asked, "And how did you sleep last night?" The girl frowned and replied, "I couldn't sleep at all. I think there must have been a stone in that bed, because I am bruised all over."

Then everyone knew the girl was a real princess, because she had felt the pea, even though it was covered by twenty mattresses and twenty eiderdowns. Only a real princess would have such sensitive skin.

So the prince had found his wife at last, and we may be sure they lived happily ever after. The pea was preserved in the royal museum, where one day you may find it, if it hasn't been stolen.

And this story, like the princess, was a real one.

The End